For Sarah
SMcB

For Eggert, the love of my life
LÓ

First US edition 2021

Library of Congress Catalog Card Number pending
ISBN 978-1-5362-1281-5

20 21 22 23 24 25 CCP 10 9 8 7 6 5 4 3 2 1

Printed in Shenzhen, Guangdong, China

This book was typeset in Brioso Pro.
The illustrations were done in mixed media.

Candlewick Press
99 Dover Street
Somerville, Massachusetts 02144

www.candlewick.com

# Mindi
### and the Goose No One Else Could See

Sam McBratney

*illustrated by*

Linda Ólafsdóttir

CANDLEWICK PRESS

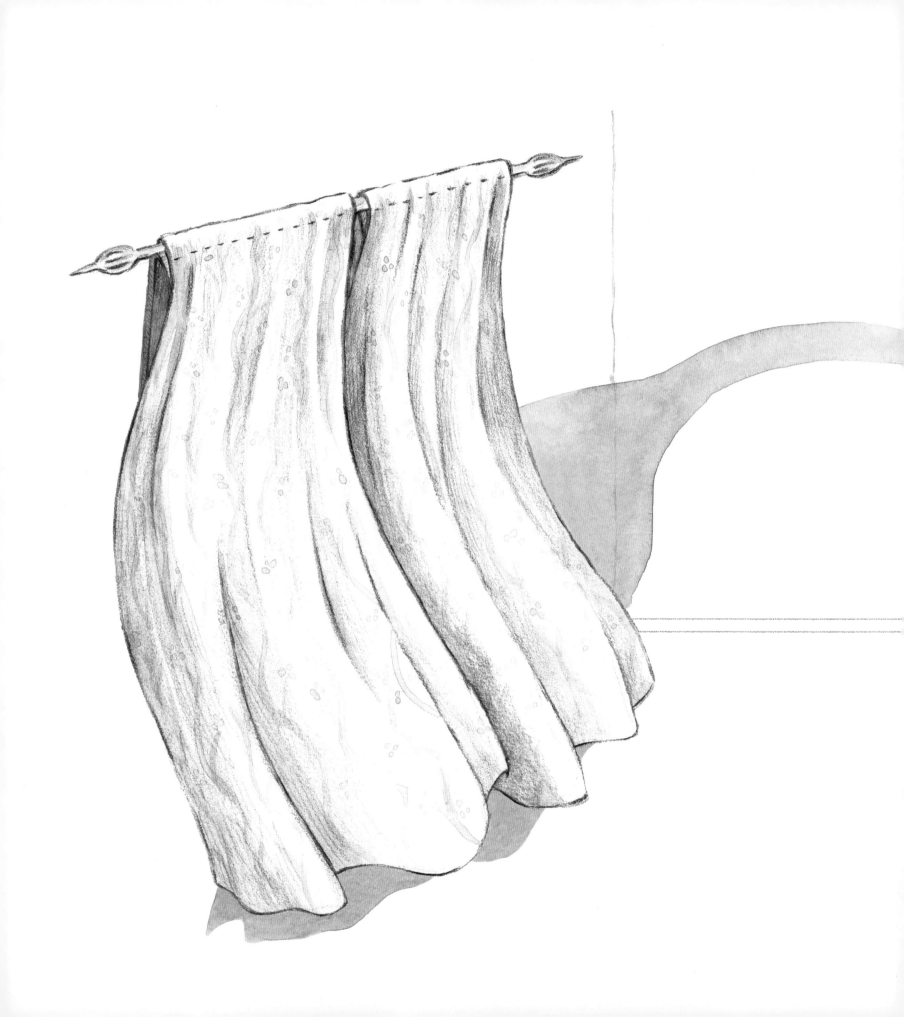

Once there was a girl named Mindi who was afraid of

something that no one else could see.

This thing that she was afraid of, this thing that

no one else could see, was a big goose.

It came into her room as quietly as a thought comes into your head,

and it stayed there for as long as it wanted to.

When she told her dad about it, he said,

"A what? There's a goose in your *room*?"

He searched high and low for the big goose,

but he could not find it.

Mindi's mom made fun
of it. She waved a wooden
spoon above her head
and said, "Any goose that
comes in here will get a smack on his silly bottom!"
Mindi thought the big goose might be
angry about the wooden spoon.
Mom and Dad shut her window tight, but windows, walls, and
doors couldn't stop the big goose. It came and stayed as usual.

"It isn't real, my love," her mom said.

"Nobody has a goose in their room."

"I do," said Mindi.

"Well, you'll just have to close your eyes and make it *not* real!"

That night, as Mindi slept between her mommy and daddy,

her mom whispered to her dad, "We have a problem, you know.

How do we get rid of this awful goose?"

Mindi's father had been asking himself the same question.

He thought now of the wise old man named Austen, who had

helped many people in the village with sensible advice.

*I'll go and see him*, thought Mindi's dad.

*I'll see what he has to say about geese!*

Austen and his animals lived halfway up

the mountain called Shelling Hill.

He greeted Mindi's dad as if he were a long-remembered friend

and listened with care to the story of the big goose.

"You see what we're up against, Austen?" Mindi's dad said.

"How can we deal with the fear of what isn't actually *there*?"

At that moment, a young goat wandered over for a cuddle from Austen, who fed her an apricot. The goat swallowed the apricot but returned the hard stone to the hand of her master.

Then Austen looked up and said, "I think you should bring your Mindi to see me. Make sure she knows I live a long way away. Make sure she knows that she is going on a *journey*."

And so it happened that Mindi and her father

set off on the journey to Shelling Hill.

When they arrived, Austen had them say hello to

the animals, including his two noisy geese.

Then they went indoors for some fruit juice.

Before long, a young goat poked open the door

and wandered in as if she owned the place.

Austen passed a big juicy apricot to Mindi.

"Here," Austen said. "This is what she wants. Give it to her, and

if she likes you, she will give you back the stone. Let's see!"

The goat returned the stone into Mindi's small hand.

"What is her name?" Mindi asked.

"Oh, I have so many goats that I have run out of names.

I just call her Number Fifteen. What would you call her?"

"I would call her Black-and-Whitey," said Mindi.

"Perfect." Austen laughed. "Black-and-Whitey she shall be!"

On the way home, Mindi's dad talked

about what they had seen on Shelling Hill.

"What did you think of those two geese?" he asked carefully.

"Nice. They were nice geese." After a pause, Mindi added,

"But the BIG goose isn't nice."

It was not the answer her father wanted to hear.

A week went by, a week of heavy rainfall

and clinging mud and sticky boots.

Mindi's mom answered a knock at the door,

and there stood Austen, dripping wet.

"Come in," she said. "Such weather to be out in!"

"Sure I never miss market day," said Austen,

and in he came—himself and . . .

a goat on the end of a short rope.

Mindi recognized Black-and-Whitey at once.

"Mommy, do we have any apricots?"

"Dear me, no, just some . . . plums."

"Oh, plums will do," said Austen. "Goats are anything but fussy.

Now then, Mindi, let's see if Black-and-Whitey still likes you.

Will she give back the stone? She should, because

you gave her such a lovely name."

There was more than one plum, and therefore more than one stone

for Mindi to accept from the goat. Suddenly she threw both arms

around Black-and-Whitey and gave her a mighty neck-squasher of a hug.

Black-and-Whitey seemed well pleased.

"Oh, yes," said Austen with a smile. "You two will be friends.
I am giving her to you, Mindi!"
Little Mindi looked at the old man with an
extraordinary shine in her eyes.

Then Austen said, "But I must have something in return. You see, it's terribly bad luck to give away an animal without getting something back, so I thought I might exchange Black-and-Whitey for the big goose that no one else can see."

He paused.

It was quite a long pause.

"Would you agree to that?"

Mindi nodded once.

"The only problem is this," said Austen. "You've been to
my cottage, so you know how far it is—what a journey! Along the
wide river, down the deep valley, and up the foggy hill. Foof! You
will not see that goose again."

Little Mindi seemed to be in deep thought

as she fed her goat the last of the plums.

And then she whispered to herself, as softly as could be,

"I love my Black-and-Whitey."

Two quick months went by. Mindi's dad went to see the wise old

man on Shelling Hill and said, "I came to thank you, Austen.

There has been no talk of a big goose since the arrival

of a certain goat—for which I must pay you."

A twinkle flickered in Austen's red-rimmed eyes.

"Oh, I've been paid well enough," he said. "Come and see."

Into the farmyard they stepped. Mindi's dad dodged the throng

of approaching goats, avoided a rooster and his ladies,

and laughed out loud as he came face-to-face with . . .

**three** thriving geese.